nickelodeon

THE LOUD HOUSE

#5 "AFTER DARK"

PAPERCUTZ™

New York

THE LOUD HOUSE

#5 "AFTER DARK"

nickelodeon THE LOUD HOUSE #5 "AFTER DARK"

"GHOST OF THE TOWN"
Sammie Crowley—Writer
Ari Castleton—Artist
Gabrielle Dolbey—Colorist
Ida Hem—Letterer

"DRAWING A PRANK"
Andrew Brooks—Writer
David Teas—Artist, Colorist
Ida Hem—Letterer

"MIDNIGHT MELODY"
Hannah Watanabe-Rocco—
Writer, Artist, Colorist
Ida Hem—Letterer

"GOAL-ORIENTED"
Andrew Brooks—Writer
Gabrielle Dolbey—Artist, Colorist
Ida Hem—Letterer

"GHOST IN THE BASEMENT"
Sammie Crowley—Writer
Ari Castleton—Artist
Gabrielle Dolbey—Colorist
Ida Hem—Letterer

"THE EARLY BIRDS AND THE WORMS"
Kevin Sullivan—Writer
Ida Hem—Artist, Letterer
Hallie Wilson—Colorist

"SHIPS IN THE NIGHT"
Sammie Crowley—Writer
Gizelle Orbino (Lisa's room), Marcus
Velazquez (Dream sequence)—Artists,
Colorists
Ida Hem—Letterer

"BUSTED!"
Sammie Crowley—Writer
Ari Castleton—Artist
Gabrielle Dolbey—Colorist
Ida Hem—Letterer

"THE PRINCESS AND THE PLEA"
Hannah Watanabe-Rocco—Writer
Isaiah Kim—Artist
Lauren Patterson—Colorist
Ida Hem—Letterer

"TUB TIME"
Kevin Sullivan—Writer
Ashley Kliment—Artist, Letterer
Colton Davis—Colorist
Ida Hem—Letterer

"BOYS IN THE ATTIC"
Sammie Crowley—Writer
Ari Castleton—Artist
Gabrielle Dolbey—Colorist
Ida Hem—Letterer

"BREAKFAST IS READY!"
Kevin Sullivan—Writer
Angela Entzminger—Artist, Colorist
Ida Hem—Letterer

JARED MORGAN—Cover Artist
JORDAN ROSATO—Endpapers
JAMES SALERNO—Sr. Art Director/Nickelodeon
JAYJAY JACKSON—Design
SEAN GANTKA, ANGELA ENTZMINGER, SAMMIE CROWLEY, DANA CLUVERIUS, MOLLIE FREILICH,
AMANDA RYNDA, MIGUEL PUGA, DIEM DOAN, DAWN GUZZO—Special Thanks
JEFF WHITMAN—Editor
JOAN HILTY—Comics Editor/Nickelodeon
JIM SALICRUP
Editor-in-Chief

ISBN: 978-1-5458-0154-3 paperback edition
ISBN: 978-1-5458-0153-6 hardcover edition

Printed in India
November 2018

Distributed by Macmillan
First Printing

MEET THE LOUD FAMILY and friends!

LINCOLN LOUD
THE MIDDLE CHILD (11)

At 11 years old, Lincoln is the middle child, with five older sisters and five younger sisters. He has learned that surviving the Loud household means staying a step ahead. He's the man with a plan, always coming up with a way to get what he wants or deal with a problem, even if things inevitably go wrong. Being the only boy comes with some perks. Lincoln gets his own room – even if it's just a converted linen closet. On the other hand, being the only boy also means he sometimes gets a little too much attention from his sisters. They mother him, tease him, and use him as the occasional lab rat or fashion show participant. Lincoln's sisters may drive him crazy, but he loves them and is always willing to help out if they need him.

LORI LOUD
THE OLDEST (17)

As the first-born child of the Loud clan, Lori sees herself as the boss of all her siblings. She feels she's paved the way for them and deserves extra respect. Her signature traits are rolling her eyes, texting her boyfriend Bobby, and literally saying "literally" all the time. Because she's the oldest and most experienced sibling, Lori can be a great ally, so it pays to stay on her good side.

LENI LOUD
THE FASHIONISTA (16)

Leni spends most of her time designing outfits and accessorizing. She always falls for Luan's pranks, and sometimes walks into walls when she's talking (she's not great at doing two things at once). Leni might be flighty, but she's the sweetest of the Loud siblings and truly has a heart of gold (even though she's pretty sure it's a heart of blood).

LUNA LOUD
THE ROCK STAR (15)

Luna is loud, boisterous and freewheeling, and her energy is always cranked to 11. She thinks about music so much that she even talks in song lyrics. On the off-chance she doesn't have her guitar with her, everything can and will be turned into a musical instrument. You can always count on Luna to help out, and she'll do most anything you ask, as long as you're okay with her supplying a rocking guitar accompaniment.

LUAN LOUD
THE JOKESTER (14)

Luan's a standup comedienne who provides a nonstop barrage of silly puns. She's big on prop comedy too – squirting flowers and whoopee cushions – so you have to be on your toes whenever she's around. She loves to pull pranks and is a really good ventriloquist – she is often found doing bits with her dummy, Mr. Coconuts. Luan never lets anything get her down; to her, laughter IS the best medicine.

LYNN LOUD
THE ATHLETE (13)

Lynn is athletic and full of energy and is always looking for a teammate. With her, it's all sports all the time. She'll turn anything into a sport. Putting away eggs? Jump shot! Score! Cleaning up the eggs? Slap shot! Score! Lynn is very competitive, tends to be superstitious about her teams, and accepts almost any dare.

LUCY LOUD
THE EMO (8)

You can always count on Lucy to give the morbid point of view in any given situation. She is obsessed with all things spooky and dark – funerals, vampires, séances, and the like. She wears mostly black and writes moody poetry. She's usually quiet and keeps to herself. Lucy has a way of mysteriously appearing out of nowhere, and try as they might, her siblings never get used to this.

LOLA LOUD
THE BEAUTY QUEEN (6)

Lola could not be more different from her twin sister, Lana. She's a pageant powerhouse whose interests include glitter, photo shoots, and her own beautiful, beautiful face. But don't let her cute, gap-toothed smile fool you; underneath all the sugar and spice lurks a Machiavellian mastermind. Whatever Lola wants, Lola gets – or else. She's the eyes and ears of the household and never resists an opportunity to tattle on troublemakers. But if you stay on Lola's good side, you've got yourself a fierce ally – and a lifetime supply of free makeovers.

LANA LOUD
THE TOMBOY (6)

Lana is the rough-and-tumble sparkplug counterpart to her twin sister, Lola. She's all about reptiles, mud pies, and muffler repair. She's the resident Ms. Fix-it and is always ready to lend a hand – the dirtier the job, the better. Need your toilet unclogged? Snake fed? Back-zit popped? Lana's your gal. All she asks in return is a little A-B-C gum, or a handful of kibble (she often sneaks it from the dog bowl).

LISA LOUD
THE GENIUS (4)

Lisa is smarter than the rest of her siblings combined. She'll most likely be a rocket scientist, or a brain surgeon, or an evil genius who takes over the world. Lisa spends most of her time working in her lab (the family has gotten used to the explosions), and says her research leaves little time for frivolous human pursuits like "playing" or "getting haircuts." That said, she's always there to help with a homework question, or to explain why the sky is blue, or to point out the structural flaws in someone's pillow fort. Lisa says it's the least she can do for her favorite test subjects, er, siblings.

LILY LOUD
THE BABY (15 MONTHS)

Lily is a giggly, drooly, diaper-ditching free spirit, affectionately known as "the poop machine." You can't keep a nappy on this kid – she's like a teething Houdini. But even when Lily's running wild, dropping rancid diaper bombs, or drooling all over the remote, she always brings a smile to everyone's face (and a clothespin to their nose). Lily is everyone's favorite little buddy, and the whole family loves her unconditionally.

RITA LOUD

Mother to the eleven Loud kids, Mom (Rita Loud) wears many different hats. She's a chauffeur, homework-checker and barf-cleaner-upper all rolled into one. She's always there for her kids and ready to jump into action during a crisis, whether it's a fight between the twins or Leni's missing shoe. When she's not chasing the kids around or at her day job as a dental hygienist, Mom pursues her passion: writing. She also loves taking on house projects and is very handy with tools (guess that's where Lana gets it from). Between writing, working, and being a mom, her days are always hectic but she wouldn't have it any other way.

LYNN LOUD SR.

Dad (Lynn Loud Sr.) is a fun-loving, upbeat aspiring chef. A kid-at-heart, he's not above taking part in the kids' zany schemes. In addition to cooking, Dad loves his van, playing the cowbell, and making puns. Before meeting Mom, Dad spent a semester in England and has been obsessed with British culture ever since — and sometimes "accidentally" slips into a British accent. When Dad's not wrangling the kids, he's pursuing his dream of opening his own restaurant where he hopes to make his "Lynn-sagnas" world-famous.

FANGS

WALT

BITEY

HOPS

GEO

CLIFF

CHARLES

CLYDE McBRIDE
THE BEST FRIEND (11)

Clyde is Lincoln's partner in crime. He's always willing to go along with Lincoln's crazy schemes (even if he sees the flaws in them up front). Lincoln and Clyde are two peas in a pod and share pretty much all of the same tastes in movies, comics, TV shows, toys – you name it. As an only child, Clyde envies Lincoln – how cool would it be to always have siblings around to talk to? But since Clyde spends so much time at the Loud household, he's almost an honorary sibling anyway. He also has a major crush on Lori.

SAM SHARP

Sam, 15, is Luna's classmate and good friend, who Luna has a crush on. Sam is all about the music – she loves to play guitar and write and compose music. Her favorite genre is rock and roll but she appreciates all good tunes. Unlike Luna, Sam only has one sibling, Simon, but she thinks even one provides enough chaos for her.

MR. BUD GROUSE

Mr. Grouse is the Louds's next-door-neighbor. The Louds often go to him for favors which he normally rejects – unless there's a chance for him to score one of Dad's famous Lynn-sagnas. Mr. Grouse loves gardening, relaxing in his recliner, and keeping anything of the Louds's that flies into his yard (his catchphrase, after all, is "my yard, my property!").

10:55 PM

WHOA, *LINCOLN!* A BLANKET FORT? THIS IS *AWESOME.*

AND, I'VE INVITED A SPECIAL GUEST TO TELL US A SPOOKY STORY...

HELLO, *CLYDE.*

EEK!

⋛YAH!⋛ *LUCY!* YOU SCARED ME!

THANKS. NOW, ONTO TONIGHT'S TALE... IT'S KNOWN AS THE SCARIEST STORY OF ALL TIME. WHAT MAKES THIS STORY ESPECIALLY SCARY?

"IT HAPPENED RIGHT HERE... IN THIS VERY HOUSE...

"A LONG TIME AGO, THERE WAS A MAN NAMED *GREGORY GARFUNKEL.* HE STUMBLED ONTO THE MOST BEAUTIFUL PLOT OF LAND IN ROYAL WOODS.

"GREGORY SET OUT TO BUILD HIS DREAM HOUSE.

"HE WAS DETERMINED TO BUILD IT ALL ON HIS OWN.

"HE STAYED UP NIGHT AFTER NIGHT, DESPERATELY TRYING TO COMPLETE HIS MASTERPIECE.

"ONCE THE HOUSE WAS FINISHED, GREGORY WAS AWED BY ITS BEAUTY.

"BUT..."

...HE WAS ABOUT TO REALIZE SOMETHING WAS AMISS...

:SQUEAK:

"GREGORY WAS CERTAIN HE'D HEARD A MOUSE.

"GREGORY SEARCHED HIGH AND LOW, ALL THROUGH THE HOUSE.

"EVERYWHERE HE WENT, HE HEARD A SQUEAK. BUT HE COULD NEVER FIND THE MOUSE.

"GREGORY STARTED TO WORRY IT WAS ALL IN HIS HEAD. HE WAS SLEEP-DEPRIVED, AFTER ALL.

"CERTAIN THERE MUST BE A MOUSE SOME-WHERE, GREGORY SET A TRAP... CAREFULLY LAYING STICKY PAPER ALL OVER THE FLOOR.

"BUT GREGORY HAD MADE A GRAVE MISTAKE. HE HADN'T PLANNED A WAY OUT.

"GREGORY TRIED TO TRAVERSE THE STICKY PAPER...

"BUT IT IMMEDIATELY ENSNARED HIM...

"GREGORY TRIED AS BEST HE COULD TO GET OUT OF THE BASEMENT...

"...BUT THE PAPER STUCK TO THE FLOOR, TRAPPING HIM.

"GREGORY NEVER LEFT THAT BASEMENT...

"AND THAT'S WHY, TO THIS VERY DAY, HE STILL *HAUNTS* THIS HOUSE."

THEY SAY THAT ANYTIME YOU FIND SOMETHING STICKY IN THE LOUD HOUSE, IT'S JUST GREGORY, REMINDING YOU OF THE TRAGIC FATE HE MET HERE.

...

THAT STORY WASN'T SCARY, LUCE!

YEAH! STICKY PAPER? THAT'S SO *LAME*.

THANKS FOR THE STORY THOUGH. IT WAS FUN.

ANY TIME.

WOOSH

"11:00 PM: DRAWING A PRANK"

AIR FLAIR

AND NOW, FOR THE FINAL PRANK OF THE EVENING...

CREEEEAAK...

WHO'S THERE?

AHHH!

EVEN WITH PRANKS, THERE'S ALWAYS A *CATCH*.

HMM... THIS *STICKY* SITUATION GIVES ME AN IDEA... ONE MORE PRANK!

END.

"12:00 AM: MIDNIGHT MELODY"

12:00 AM

THE WAY I FEEL ABOUT YOU IS OUT OF THIS ♪ WORLD, ♪

'CAUSE YOU'RE SO COOL THAT YOU'VE ♪ GOTTA BE--

WHAT RHYMES WITH "WORLD"?

≈GASP!≈

SLAM

MR. WINKY BEAR? WHERE'S MR. WINKY BEAR?

SHHH! DUDE, YOU'RE SLEEPWALKING AGAIN.

I'VE GOT TO GET TO THE ATTIC TO SAVE MR. WINKY BEAR!

YOU HAVEN'T PLAYED WITH HIM SINCE YOU WERE FIVE!

THE ATTIC... AND MR. WINKY BEAR... ARE THAT-A-WAY.

HOW DID LUAN SLEEP THROUGH ALL OF THAT?

ZZZZ

THE WAY I FEEL ABOUT YOU IS OUT OF THIS WORLD, 'CAUSE YOU'RE SO COOL THAT YOU'VE GOTTA BE--

CURLED? HURLED? TWIRLED? ≥ARGH!≤

SHOULD I CALL SAM?

WHAT IF SHE'S ASLEEP? WHAT IF SHE THINKS I'M A TOTAL WEIRDO? WHAT IF SHE'S ASLEEP *AND* THINKS I'M A TOTAL WEIRDO?!

RING RING RING

HELLO?

HEY, SAM! YOU MUST THINK I'M A WEIRDO FOR CALLING SO LATE...

NOT AT ALL! I WAS UP ANYWAY BINGING THAT AWESOME NEW COOKING COMPETITION SHOW, "COOKING A MEAL IN THIRTY SECONDS WHILE SUSPENDED FORTY FEET ABOVE A PIT OF HOT LAVA." WHAT'S UP?

I HAD A DREAM ABOUT THE BEST SONG EVER SO I WOKE UP AND STARTED WRITING IT, BUT NOW I CAN'T FIND A WORD THAT RHYMES WITH "WORLD" AND IT'S REALLY KILLIN' MY VIBE.

OH, MAN, THAT HAPPENS TO ME WHEN I WRITE SONGS TOO! BUT THEN I'M LIKE, WHAT'S MORE PUNK THAN MAKING LYRICS *NOT* RHYME?

"2:00 AM: THE EARLY BIRDS AND THE WORMS"

32

MAKES SENSE. BYEEEEE!

≈SIGH≈

THERE! THAT'S ALL OF THEM. LETS GO, HOPS.

ALL RIGHT, IT'S PARTY TIME! EDDIE, GRAB THE CHIPS.

I'M PHIL!

WE'VE GOT TO START WEARING NAME TAGS.

END.

HUH. LIMITED BRAINWAVES. SHE MUST NOT BE HAVING ANY DREAMS TONIGHT.

OOOH! LENI'S SLEEPWALKING AGAIN!

⇒SQUEE!⇐ I'VE GOT TO ADD HER TO MY STUDY!

END.

WILL THE SEARCH FOR GREGORY CONTINUE AFTER CLYDE'S HUNGER IS SATISFIED? STAY TUNED...

4:00 AM

=GRRR!=

LANA, THERE'S SOMETHING UNDER MY MATTRESS AND IT FEELS ALL WEIRD AND LUMPY AND I CAN'T SLEEP!

LANAAAAA, WHERE ARE YOU?!

LANA?!

52

53

6:00 AM

CLIFF, I THINK MY SNORING DROVE DAD TO SLEEP IN THE ATTIC LAST NIGHT.

BLOOP

SO I'M COOKING BREAKFAST TODAY TO MAKE IT UP TO HIM.

THAT WAY HE CAN SLEEP A LITTLE LONGER AND BE EXTRA RELAXED THIS MORNING.

SIZZLE

DUMB LUAN PRANK... FREEZING WATER... WASTED BATH BALL...

I DON'T THINK I SHOULD EVEN ASK WHAT THAT WAS ABOUT...

⸗SLURP!⸗
⸗SLURP!⸗

⸗BRRR!⸗

WATCH OUT FOR PAPERCUTZ

Back in THE LOUD HOUSE #3, we mentioned that THE LOUD HOUSE #4, the next graphic novel would be entitled "The Struggle is Real," and as all true THE LOUD HOUSE graphic novel fans already know, THE LOUD HOUSE #4 was actually entitled "Family Tree." So you might be wondering, what happened?

Here's what happened: When we got word that THE LOUD HOUSE ULTIMATE TREEHOUSE app was coming, we just couldn't wait to tell you, but it was still TOP SECRET! Oh, sure we suddenly changed the title, whipped up a new cover featuring a treehouse, and even added an all-new story featuring Lincoln building a treehouse, and added a gazillion tree-references into the Watch Out for Papercutz page, but we never spilled the beans! We promised to reveal what all the tree-talk was about in THE LOUD HOUSE #5, but we did say you'd find out faster on Instagram at @TheLoudHouseCartoon and on Facebook.com/TheLoudHouse, and we're sure you did! If you've been playing THE LOUD HOUSE ULTIMATE TREEHOUSE game, we're also sure you can see why we were so excited.

Meanwhile, we had yet another crazy idea! We usually do short stories for each graphic novel because we've been working with the super-talented writers and artists from THE LOUD HOUSE show itself, and they don't have time to do much more than a short comics story while they're busy working on the animated TV series.

But what if we came up with an overall theme, like the entire graphic novel taking place over the course of a single night in THE LOUD HOUSE? It would still be a bunch of fun short stories, but when presented altogether it could feel like one big story, right? That's how we came up with THE LOUD HOUSE #5 "After Dark," where we've explored all that goes bump in the night (not just Leni sleepwalking) in Lincoln's home. We hope you enjoyed it. Now, what crazy ideas will we come up with for LOUD HOUSE #6? There's only one way to find out, and that's to be sure to look for THE LOUD HOUSE #6, coming soon!

Thanks!

Jim

STAY IN TOUCH!

EMAIL: salicrup@papercutz.com
WEB: papercutz.com
TWITTER: @papercutzgn
INSTAGRAM: @papercutzgn
FACEBOOK: PAPERCUTZGRAPHICNOVELS
FANMAIL: Papercutz, 160 Broadway, Suite 700,
               East Wing, New York, NY 10038

Eric Esquivel–Writer, David DeGrand–Artist, Laurie E. Smith & Matt Herms–Colorists, Tom Orzechowski–Letterer

Pick up NICKELODEON PANDEMONIUM! #3 for the hair-raising conclusion, plus more stories from THE LOUD HOUSE!

LIVE LOUD!

THE LOUD HOUSE
ULTIMATE TREEHOUSE APP

Build the ultimate towering tree house with **Lincoln Loud**!

Free to download on Apple and Android devices.

THE LOUD HOUSE
LISTEN OUT LOUD PODCAST

Get ready to hang with **The Loud House** family like never before!

Listen to new episodes of their podcast, **Listen Out Loud**, on all podcast apps, Nickelodeon's YouTube channel or the Nick App!